Animals Aboard!

Andrew Fusek Peters

Illustrated by Jim Coplestone

F

FRANCES LINCOLN
CHILDREN'S BOOKS

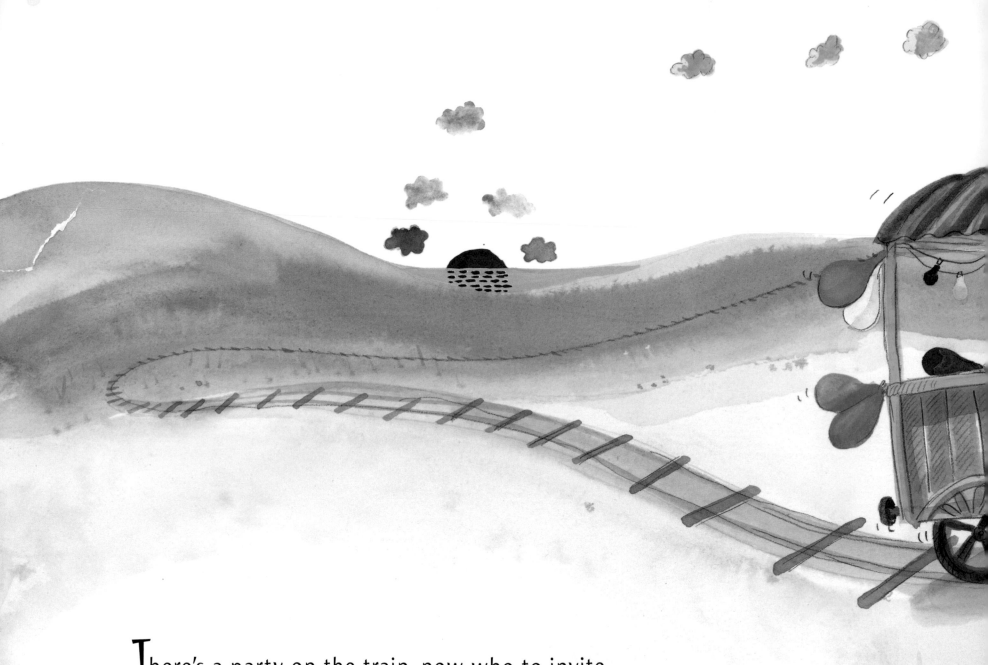

There's a party on the train, now who to invite
To climb aboard and dance through the night?

The train arrives with a

Choo!
Choo!
Choo!

And Cow jumps on with a

Moo! Moo!
Moo!

As they head on down that clackety track,
Duck waddles on with a
Quack!
Quack!
Quack!

The carriages are cantering all the way,

So Horse leaps up with a

Neigh! Neigh! Neigh!

Round and round like a spinning wheel,
Pig flies on with a Squeal! Squeal! Squeal!

Trickety-tickety, the best of luck,
Now Hen stomps on with a

Cluck!
Cluck!
Cluck!

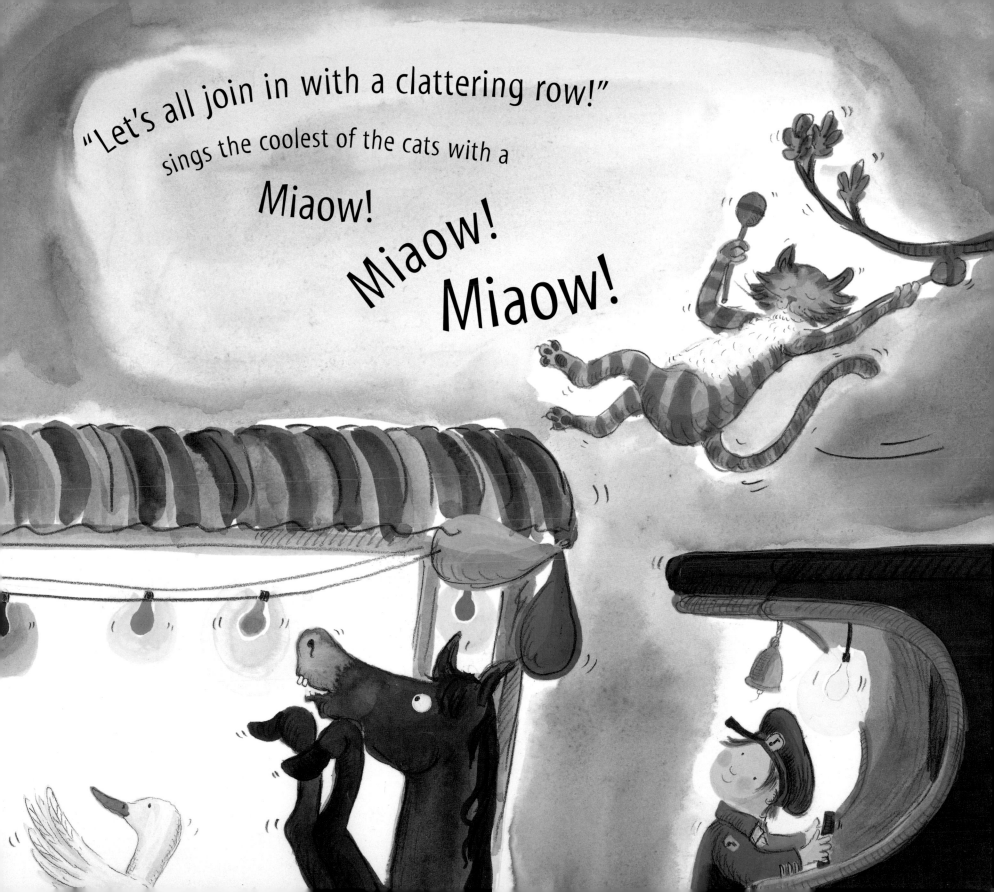

Time for a dance, *yes*, clap to that song

As the train like a rattlesnake moves along.

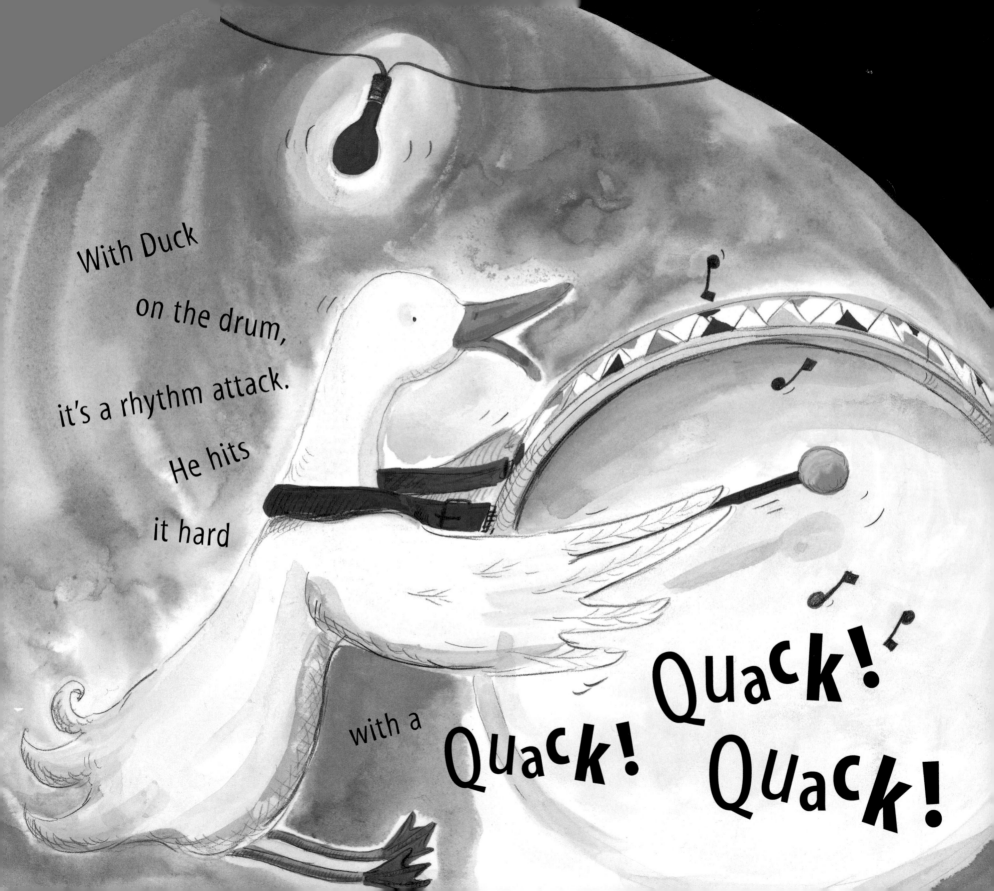

Bopping and popping with such appeal

It's Pig on sax with a Squeal! Squeal! Squeal!

Hen goes round, she's coming unstuck
As she spins that record
with a Cluck! Cluck! Cluck!

Cat on maracas with a flourish and bow,
Tapping and slapping
with a Miaow! Miaow! Miaow!

Party animals, feeling all right,
    sighing their sound
        through the never-never night.

But the train is tired
at the end of the cruise,
And the wheels on the track
are slowing to a snooze.

Under the stars, we're counting sheep,
As we listen to the lullaby of sleep, sleep, sleep.

"Goodnight!" says the rhythm of the snoring horde,
Party's over for the Animals Aboard.

For my son Asa, who loves trains and animals and gave me the inspiration! – A.F.P.
For lovely Louis, my boy – J.C.

Animals Aboard! copyright © Frances Lincoln Limited 2007
Text copyright © Andrew Fusek Peters 2007
Illustrations copyright © Jim Coplestone 2007

First published in Great Britain and in the USA in 2007 by
Frances Lincoln Children's Books, 4 Torriano Mews,
Torriano Avenue, London NW5 2RZ

www.franceslincoln.com
Distributed in the USA by Publishers Group West

British Library Cataloguing in Publication Data available on request

ISBN: 978-1-84507-582-8

The illustrations for this book are watercolour
Printed in China

1 3 5 7 9 8 6 4 2

Find out more about the author of this book on his website: www.tallpoet.com